Stella
KEEPS THE SUN UP

Written by Clothilde Ewing   Illustrated by Lynn Gaines

A Denene Millner Book
Simon & Schuster Books for Young Readers
New York London Toronto Sydney New Delhi

SIMON & SCHUSTER BOOKS FOR YOUNG READERS
An imprint of Simon & Schuster Children's Publishing Division
1230 Avenue of the Americas, New York, New York 10020
Text © 2022 by Clothilde Ewing
Illustration © 2022 by Lynn Gaines
Book design by Lizzy Bromley © 2022 by Simon & Schuster, Inc.
For information about special discounts for bulk purchases,
please contact Simon & Schuster Special Sales at 1-866-506-1949 or business@simonandschuster.com.
The Simon & Schuster Speakers Bureau can bring authors to your live event.
For more information or to book an event, contact the Simon & Schuster Speakers Bureau at
1-866-248-3049 or visit our website at www.simonspeakers.com.
The text for this book was set in Limes Sans.
The illustrations for this book were rendered in Photoshop.
Manufactured in China · 1221 SCP
First Edition
2 4 6 8 10 9 7 5 3 1
Library of Congress Cataloging-in-Publication Data
Names: Ewing, Clothilde, author. | Gaines, Lynn, illustrator.
Title: Stella keeps the sun up / Clothilde Ewing ; illustrated by Lynn Gaines.
Description: First edition. | New York : Simon & Schuster Books for Young Readers, [2022] | Audience: Ages 4-8. |
Audience: Grades K-1. | Summary: "When Stella does not want to go to bed,
she tries all sorts of ways to keep the sun up"—Provided by publisher.
Identifiers: LCCN 2020039835 (print) | LCCN 2020039836 (eBook) |
ISBN 9781534487857 (hardcover) | ISBN 9781534487864 (eBook)
Subjects: CYAC: Sleep—Fiction. | Sun—Fiction.
Classification: LCC PZ7.1.E967 St 2022 (print) | LCC PZ7.1.E967 (eBook) | DDC [E]—dc23
LC record available at https://lccn.loc.gov/2020039835
LC eBook record available at https://lccn.loc.gov/2020039836

To my village,
who inspired me to believe anything is possible.
To my children,
who have reawakened in me a sense of wonder in the world.
—C. E.

Mom and Mel, my favorite cheerleaders—
may you always have sunshine!
—L. G.

Hi, I'm Stella.

My name means "star."
I don't look like a star,
but I do like to sparkle!

I am a really good jumper. And super fast. I bet I can jump high enough to kiss the moon.

If I were that high in the sky,
I would visit the sun, too.
I bet it's cozy up there.

My friend Kamrynn loves to be cozy too.

She used to live next door, but her family moved away.
Now she lives on the other side of the world.

Want to know
something cool?
When I wake up
in the morning,

Kamrynn is
getting ready
to go to bed!

I wish I didn't have to go to sleep. It's *so* boring.
If I could make the rules, here's what they would be:

1. Dessert comes
   before dinner.

2. Pajamas are
for all the time,
not just bedtime.

And . . .

3. On our sixth birthday, we can stop sleeping.

My buddy
Roger
agrees.

Why do we have to miss all the fun and go to bed just because it gets dark? he asks. *It's all the sun's fault.*

Roger is onto something.

If it never gets dark, then we can stay awake forever! All we have to do is keep the sun up.

Simple! We'll start tomorrow.

Rise and shine!

I brush my teeth twice as long . . . since I won't
have to brush them later before bed.

I put on plenty
of sunscreen . . .

and I grab my
supersize sunglasses.

Now all we have to do is play
it cool, so Mom and Dad don't
figure out the plan.

"Good morning!" I say. "Roger and I got a great night's sleep. Did I tell you Roger snores? Anyway, we just slept—no talking—so you have nothing to worry about."

Uh-oh. Roger is going to give us away.

"This cereal is delicious." *Sluuuuuuurp!*

"Stella, what's going on?" Dad asks.
"Sorry, gotta go. I'm late for work," I say.

I run through the house and stuff my backpack with everything we'll need.

Save some room for me!
Roger shouts.

"Better get comfy, Sun. You're going to be up for a while."

If we are loud enough, maybe we can keep the sun awake.

If we shine lights at the sun, maybe it will keep shining back!

If we keep doing our morning yoga, maybe it will get confused about what time it is.

If we send it an invitation, maybe the sun will stay up and party with us.

Our plan seems to be working.
But Roger is worried.

*Are we going to have to
stand in this exact spot
and do all these things
for the rest of our lives to
keep the sun up?* he asks.

I spend so long thinking
about this, the sun drops
low in the sky.

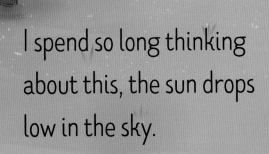

I pull Roger into the kitchen
and pour him a bowl of cereal.
Cereal again? Roger complains.

"Shhhhhhhh," I say. "If we eat cereal,
the sun will think it's still morning.
Let's also give the sun that drink
Mom sips to help her wake up."

*How are we going to get a cup
of coffee all the way up there?*
Roger asks.

Are we there yet?
Roger asks.

"I think we are too
heavy," I say.

Trampoline? Roger asks.

"Probably not a good idea."

This is a disaster.

The sun is tougher
than I thought.

Good thing we're just getting warmed up.

Before we know it, Mom is shouting,
"Stella, time for dinner!"
It can't be that time already!
After dinner comes a bath . . .
and after a bath comes books . . .
and after books comes . . .

NoOoooo!

"Do we have to eat dinner this exact second?" I ask.

"Stella, this isn't a negotiation," Mom says. "I'm counting to five." She sounds serious.

"Roger, you stay here. Don't let the sun out of your sight."

At dinner, I am too worried to eat. Roger is not
tough enough to take on the sun on his own.
I wish Kamrynn were here to help.
And then it hits me!
We have been thinking about this all wrong!
I shovel some broccoli and chicken into my mouth
and try to find Roger before it's too late.

"Roger, we have to go to bed now!"
*But we have been trying to keep the
sun awake all day. Why would we
give up now?* he asks.

"Kamrynn is waiting for
us to go to sleep! If we
keep the sun up here, she
will be stuck in bed for a
hundred years!"

That would be terrible.
We better let the sun go, then, Roger says sadly.

We take one last look at the sun. It has nearly set. "Thanks for a fun day," I say. "Tell Kamrynn I said, 'Hi.'"

At bedtime, Mom and Dad read a story and tuck in Roger and me. And then, it is time for sleep.

"Good night, Roger," I whisper.
Good night, Stella. Sleep tight,
Roger whispers back.
"Good night, Sun. See you in the
morning!" we whisper together.